Tell Someone

Debra Kempf Shumaker

illustrated by Tristan Yuvienco

Albert Whitman & Company
Chicago, Illinois

When I'm bumped and bruised

or scraped and scratched—

if I'm hurt—

I tell someone.

Telling someone helps make it better.

When I pedal real fast

and stay upright—

if I'm happy—

I tell someone.

High fives all around!

If Murphy is missing

and my tears won't stop—

when I'm worried—

I tell someone.

Two are better than one.

When my heart feels full

and I hug real tight—

when I'm grateful—

it feels so good to tell everyone!

If my best friend moves

and my day seems empty—

when I feel all alone—

I tell someone.

Sometimes a hug is just the thing I need.

If the first day of school
makes my stomach feel funny—
when I'm nervous—

I tell someone.

They might feel the same way.

When I take a BIG step
and I say, "Hello"—
when I'm brave—

I tell someone.

It feels good to do hard things.

If I pick a fight

or laugh and make fun—

when I know I'm wrong—

I tell them I'm sorry.

It's the right thing to do.

And I feel better too.

If I'm foot-stomping,

fist-clenching,

I-could-cry mad—

I tell someone.

Saying my feelings out loud helps me calm down.

When I miss Grandma

and her huge, huge hugs—

if I am sad—

I tell Grandpa.

Sharing memories makes us both smile.

If kids block my way

or grab my stuff—

if they laugh and make me feel small—

when I'm afraid—

I tell someone.

Some things I can't fix by myself.

If I have a secret that doesn't feel right,

or someone makes me feel weird or wrong inside—

it might be scary, but—

I tell someone.

A grown-up I trust can help me.

Whether I'm happy or proud;

confused or hurt (inside or out);

worried, mad, or sad;

or just all mixed-up inside—

I know I am able to help myself...

if—

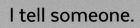

I tell someone.

A Note to Parents and Caregivers

Parents and caregivers have opportunities each day to encourage, empower, and model appropriate behaviors for children. Creating a foundation of open communication is essential in helping youth develop healthy ways to process the world around them, form deep connections, and avoid dangerous or hurtful situations. If children are to open up and disclose potentially sensitive information, it is critical that they feel they can talk to an adult they trust.

Our kids' lived experiences are important and unique and deserve our full attention. When a child is sharing with us, we can reinforce productive discourse by listening with our whole bodies—putting down electronics, making eye contact, facing the child, turning our bodies to lean into the conversation, repeating what we are hearing, not cutting them off or jumping to a conclusion or solution, and prompting the child to express their feelings or emotions.

There are fundamental differences between *telling* and *tattling*. For caregivers or those who work with children, tattling can be an exhausting and time-consuming behavior that hinders productivity and interferes with building quality relationships. On the other hand, telling is an essential way to connect with your child, possibly discover a true emergency, or address a hazard or trauma. Encouraging kids to pause to ask themselves a few questions can be a great way to help them think about whether they are telling (important or urgent information) or tattling (not important or urgent information).

Children should be assured that their minds, bodies, encounters, and voices matter. Our hope is that this book helps you start empowering discussions, about trust, safety, and belonging, with the kids in your life.

Ashley Rhodes-Courter
Clinical social worker, speaker, and
author of the *New York Times* bestseller
Three Little Words and *Sam Is My Sister*

To Sharon—sharing your memories makes us all smile.—DKS

To Annette, and to the Renato and Vergara-Constantino families!—TY

Library of Congress Cataloging-in-Publication data
is on file with the publisher.

Text copyright © 2021 by Debra Kempf Shumaker
Illustrations copyright © 2021 by Albert Whitman & Company
Illustrations by Tristan Yuvienco
First published in the United States of America in 2021 by Albert Whitman & Company
ISBN 978-0-8075-7769-1 (hardcover)
ISBN 978-0-8075-7772-1 (ebook)

Printed in China
10 9 8 7 6 5 4 3 2 1 WKT 26 25 24 23 22 21

Design by Valerie Hernández

For more information about Albert Whitman & Company,
visit our website at www.albertwhitman.com.